T5-DHH-941

FAST BREAK!

Tristan Howard

A
LITTLE **APPLE**
PAPERBACK

SCHOLASTIC INC.
New York Toronto London Auckland Sydney

*For Matt and Lucy, the coolest guys
we know. . . .*

M. P.
D. W.

If you purchased this book without a cover, you should be aware that this book is stolen property. It was reported as "unsold and destroyed" to the publisher, and neither the author nor the publisher has received any payment for this "stripped book."

No part of this publication may be reproduced in whole or in part, or stored in a retrieval system, or transmitted in any form or by any means, electronic, mechanical, photocopying, recording, or otherwise, without written permission of the publisher. For information regarding permission, write to Scholastic Inc., 555 Broadway, New York, NY 10012.

ISBN 0-590-96219-1

Copyright © 1997 by Daniel Weiss Associates, Inc. Conceived by Edward Monagle, Michael Pollack, and Daniel Weiss. Grateful acknowledgment to Stephen Currie. All rights reserved. Published by Scholastic Inc. LITTLE APPLE PAPERBACKS and the LITTLE APPLE PAPERBACKS logo are trademarks of Scholastic Inc. Cover art copyright © 1997 by Daniel Weiss Associates, Inc. Interior illustrations by Marcy Ramsey.

Produced by Daniel Weiss Associates, Inc.
33 West 17th Street, New York, NY 10011

12 11 10 9 8 7 6 5 4 3 2 1   7 8 9/9 0 1/0

Printed in the U.S.A.   40

First Scholastic printing, February 1997

ATLANTIC COUNTY LIBRARY

Chapter

1

"Catherine! Pass it to me!"

Adam Fingerhut stood on the basketball court, waving his arms like crazy.

"No!" Matt Carter thumped his chest. "I'm the star!" he shouted. "Pass it to me!"

"No way!" Adam turned toward Matt. "I'm better than you!"

I threw the ball to Adam. He could have caught it. He *should* have caught it. But he never saw it. I guess he was too busy yelling at Matt. The ball hit him right in the stomach.

And Adam has kind of a lot of stomach.

He fell to the floor. "Oof!" he said.

"I *told* you to pass it to me," Matt said, and rolled his eyes.

"I'll be okay." Adam stood up slowly and took a deep breath. "Boy, basketballs are hard!" he said.

"Let's shoot!" Matt suggested. He dribbled the ball toward me. I tried to grab it away from him. "You're dead meat, Matt!" I shouted.

But Matt just giggled and turned around in one quick move. Now he was dribbling with his back toward me. He reached out with his elbow so I couldn't get past. "Who's dead meat?" he asked.

"You are!" I yelled. I tried to sneak around Matt's other side, hoping he wouldn't see me. My fingers stretched out for the ball. . . .

But Matt was too fast for me. He dribbled right past where I'd just been standing.

"No fair!" I said. But I had to admit, it was a great move.

Matt tossed the ball up and into the basket. He's tall, so it wasn't too hard. "Two points!" he shouted with

a grin. Then he stuck out his chest as if he were someone really important. "No autographs, please."

Tweet! My mother blew her whistle.

3

She's our coach. "Over here, team!" she called.

We ran to the bench as fast as we could. When we got near Mom, Mitchell Rubin and I both slid across the floor on our bottoms. "Safe!" Mitchell yelled.

"Don't be silly." Julie Zimmer frowned at us. "This isn't baseball. It's basketball."

"It *is*?" Mitchell put a goofy grin on his face. "Gee, thanks for telling me," he said. "I didn't know that."

Julie just sighed.

Our team is called the Rangers, but everyone calls us the Leftovers. We're the players that nobody else wanted. Alex Slavik has feet so big he trips over them. Brenda Bailey's favorite part of the games is the food afterward. And Mitchell says he gets messages

4

from aliens—by listening to his shoes!

In the spring we play baseball, and in the fall we play soccer. But today was our first practice of basketball season. My name is Catherine Antler. I'm in third grade.

"The first thing we'll learn," Mom said, "is how to dribble a basketball."

"Aw, Mrs. Antler," Matt said. "Can't we shoot?"

"Later," Mom told him. She dropped the ball and let it bounce. "You put your hand out like this," she said, "and then you—ow!"

"And then you ow?" Alex looked confused. "How do you ow?"

"I had a cow and it said ow," Lucy Marcus sang.

Mom wiggled her fingers. "I said ow because the ball hit me, Alex," she told him. "Rule number one—don't put your hand out the way I did!"

I laughed. Mom doesn't really know too much about baseball or soccer. It looked as though she didn't know too much about basketball, either.

"Would somebody show us how it's done?" Mom asked.

"She means somebody should show us *ow* it's done," Mitchell whispered.

"Me!" Matt waved his hand as hard as he could. But Joanna Wrightman's hand waved even harder.

"Okay, Joanna," Mom said.

Joanna stood up proudly. Mom gave her a ball. Joanna held it with both hands, way over her head.

"You bounce it like this," she said, and threw the ball down with all her might.

It would have bounced high.

Maybe even into the basket! But it didn't—because Joanna's foot got in the way.

"Ow!" she yelled as the ball slammed onto her toes.

"Everybody on our team says ow," Mitchell chuckled. He poked me in the ribs. "Get it? Everybody on *ow*-er team?"

"Not so hard, Joanna," Mom said. "Anybody else?"

"Me!" Matt stood up. But Mom called on Yin Wong instead.

Yin dropped the ball on the floor. It bounced back up. "Tap it again, Yin!" Mom urged.

But Yin didn't. She watched it bounce again and again. Each time it bounced lower. Finally the ball stopped bouncing and rolled across the floor.

"You have to keep bouncing it, Yin," Mom explained.

Yin shrugged. "This way I won't get hurt," she said.

She was right. Already three people had gotten hurt by the basketball: Adam, Mom, and Joanna.

"Anybody else?" Mom asked.

I sat on my hands. I sure didn't want to get hurt!

This time Mom called on Matt. "Yes!" he shouted. He threw both fists into the air. He was so excited, he didn't notice that Mom was tossing him the ball.

"Look out!" Danny West called.

The big orange ball bounced right into Matt's chin. "Ow!" he shouted. He grabbed his face. "Feel my head and see if it's broken!"

"Oh, dear," Mom said. She ran over to Matt.

" 'Cause it's one, two, three strikes

you're out!'" Mitchell sang happily. "Get it—*ow-t*?"

I got it, but I didn't want to get it. I was too worried about being on a basketball team.

Basketballs weren't just big and hard—they were dangerous!

Chapter 2

In basketball, you aren't allowed to run with the ball. So we spent most of the rest of practice working on our dribbling and passing. That's how you get the ball from one place to another.

But dribbling and passing were boring. We were glad when it was finally time to shoot!

The basket is ten feet up, so it's hard for a kid to score. If you get the ball in the net, you get two points. Matt was pretty good at it. The rest of us weren't so hot.

"I can score from here," Matt boasted. He stood far away from the basket and threw the ball hard. It hit the rim and bounced away.

"Oh, yeah?" Adam glared at Matt. "I can score from *here*." He stood even farther away and shot. But the

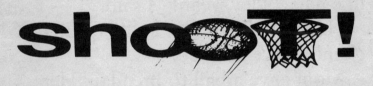

ball didn't go near the basket.

"Air ball, air ball," Matt chanted. Adam stuck out his tongue.

"What does 'air ball' mean?" Brenda asked.

"When you don't even hit the rim, that's an air ball," Matt explained.

Brenda frowned. "But every time you shoot, the ball goes in the air. So why don't you say 'air ball' every time?"

Danny scratched his head. "That's right. How come?"

"Maybe it's really 'hair ball,'" Josh Ramos suggested. "See the black lines on the ball? They look kind of like hair."

I squinted. The lines *were* a little like hair. "Hey, yeah!" I said.

"Hair ball! Hair ball!" Mitchell chanted. We grinned.

Mom gave a ball to Brenda. "Here," she said. "Try to get it in the basket."

Brenda's very short, so the basket was *way* above her head. "Here goes nothing," she said, and she threw it up into the air.

It went high enough. But it didn't go far enough. The ball fell back into Brenda's arms.

"Air ball!" Adam shouted.

"Hair ball!" Mitchell chimed in.

"Try again," Mom encouraged her.

Brenda shrugged. "Okay, Mrs. Antler," she agreed. "But I don't think it'll help."

She stepped closer to the basket and tried again. The ball went above the rim. Then down it came—back into Brenda's arms.

"Air ball!" everybody said. Except Mitchell and me. We said, "Hair ball!"

"Try shooting from right under the basket," Josh told her.

"Good idea!" Brenda stood so that the net was right above her head. She leaned back a little. Then she threw the ball up high.

"It's a last-second shot!" Danny said into a pretend microphone. "Will it go in, ladies and gentlemen, or will it be another air ball?"

The ball flew up through the net and into the air above the basket. Then it started to come down. It looked like a pumpkin spinning in the sky.

"Here it comes!" Danny said.

The ball dropped right through the net!

"And it's good!" Danny yelled. "The fans are going wild!"

"Two points!" Lucy shrieked. She did a cartwheel, and her brown pony-tail went flipping through the air.

"All right!" Brenda cheered. She jumped for joy. But as she went up, the ball fell right onto her head. There was a loud thump, and Brenda crashed to the floor.

"Are you all right?" Lucy asked.

Brenda put her hand up to her head. "I'm okay," she said. Then she grinned. "I scored two points!"

"No, you didn't." Matt shook his

head. "First you scored *minus* two points because the ball went through the basket the wrong way."

"Oh." Brenda looked sad.

"Then you scored two points when it went back through, but two points plus minus two points is zero points," Matt went on. "So you didn't score. But watch what I can do!" He faced the other end of the court. Then he leaned back and shot the ball over his head.

Wham! The ball bounced off the backboard and dropped through the hoop.

"Two points!" Matt said. "I bet nobody else can do that!"

Danny tried. So did Adam, Joanna, and Julie. But none of them came close.

"Can I try?" Alex walked over to us, trying not to trip over his feet.

"I bet the ball throws Alex into the basket," Lucy whispered as Matt handed him the ball. "Not the other way around!"

Alex leaned back. "Like this?" he asked. He looked like a big flamingo when he leaned back like that, I thought. A flamingo with bright red hair!

"Farther," Matt said.

Alex nodded. He leaned back some more—

Crash!

Alex picked himself up off the floor. He rubbed his back. "Oops," he said slowly. "I guess I leaned a little too far!"

I sighed. Already six people had gotten hurt. And only Matt had scored a basket.

At this rate, I figured, we'd never win a game!

Chapter

3

"Are we all ready?" Mom asked. She grinned.

A few of us grinned back. But most of us didn't.

It was two days later, and we were about to play our first game. The other team was the Tigers, and they were huge. They looked twenty feet tall. I poked Danny in the side. "We'll never score a point," I whispered.

"We'll have to stand on each other's

shoulders," Danny whispered back. He chewed his bubble gum hard.

I thought he was making a joke. But I wasn't sure. Maybe he was serious.

"Go, Rangers!" Mom yelled. She pumped her fist in the air.

"Go, Rangers," we all said . . . softly.

The referee threw the ball in the air. "Out of my way!" Matt yelled. He dribbled up to the basket. Then he let the ball fly. It arched into the air— and into the net.

"Go, Rangers!" we all shouted.

Matt bowed toward the bench. "Thank you, thank you!" he said.

We were leading, 2–0. Maybe it would be a good game after all, I thought. If only we could get the ball to Matt every time!

The Tigers brought the ball down the

court. "Get the ball, Julie!" I yelled.

But Julie stepped to the side, and the Tigers scored.

"Why didn't you stop them?" I yelled, frustrated.

Julie made a face. "What? And get all sweaty?"

I sighed. Did I mention that Julie cares a lot about how she looks?

Matt started to dribble, but a Tiger took the ball away from him. Matt spun around. "Hey, that was a foul!" he told the referee.

"What's a foul?" Alex asked Danny.

"It's when you hit somebody," Danny explained.

"Oh," Alex said. "I thought a foul was a kind of bird."

"That's spelled *f-o-w-l*, Alex," Lucy explained. "In basketball, it's spelled *f-o-u-l*."

A Tiger dribbled toward our basket

and jumped to shoot. "Stop him, Mitchell!" Mom called out.

Mitchell jumped high in the air. He kicked his leg out like a karate guy. *"Hi-yaah!"* he screamed.

It was a pretty good move. It was too bad we were playing basketball and not competing in a karate match.

And it was too bad Mitchell's foot hit the Tiger in the arm.

Tweet! The referee blew his whistle.

"Foul!" the referee shouted. "Tigers get two free throws."

FOUL!

"What are free throws?" Alex asked.

Josh frowned. "Um . . . a free throw is when you don't have to pay to shoot."

"Oh." Alex looked extremely worried. Even his freckles looked worried. "How much does it cost to shoot when it isn't free?" he wanted to know. "I only have fifty cents."

I bit my lip. I didn't think I could afford to shoot very many baskets.

Danny sighed. "That's not it," he said. "You get two free throws if you're fouled. They're called free because no one can block you."

"Oh, sure," Josh said. "I knew that."

Danny rolled his eyes. "And each free throw is worth only one point."

The Tigers missed both free throws, but they got the rebound. A big girl dribbled toward Joanna.

"Get the ball, Joanna!" Mom cried.

Joanna held up her hand. "Stop!" she ordered. "Our coach says it's my turn now."

22

The big girl didn't stop. She dribbled around Joanna and shot.

Swish!

Now it was Tigers 4, Rangers 2.

"No fair!" Joanna glared at the big girl. "She didn't give me the ball!"

"Next time say please," Brenda suggested.

"Time-out!" Mom called. All the kids on our team came over to the bench. "Joanna, dear, it's your job to take the ball away," she said. "And Mitchell, no more karate kicks."

Mitchell grinned. "Did you see the look on that guy's face, though?"

"This is dumb," Matt said. "I'll play by myself. One on five. One of me, five of them. The rest of you can watch."

23

"We're a team, Matt," Mom told him. She clapped her hands. "Okay, Rangers! Back to the court!"

But Matt was right about one thing: He was our best player—by a lot! The rest of us usually just gave him the ball.

Once he stole the ball away from Mitchell. "Hey!" Mitchell said. He blinked up at Matt from behind his messy hair. "We're on the same team!"

"Well, you'll *never* get a basket!" Matt replied.

Soon the score was Tigers 12, Matt 6—I mean, Rangers 6.

At the beginning of the second half, Lucy lay down on the floor.

"This game is too hard," she said. "Hey! If you put your ear to the floor, you can hear the ball bouncing."

I lay down next to her and listened. "You're right!" I said.

Lucy grinned. "This is more fun than playing."

I could hear footsteps, too. The floor shook. "Why is it getting louder?" I wondered.

Lucy sat up. Suddenly she looked frightened. "Get up, Catherine!" she yelled. "Here they come!"

I looked up. Uh-oh! A Tiger was about to run over me! "Help!" I yelled. As quickly as I could, I rolled into a little ball.

"Why don't you guys dribble somewhere else?" Lucy huffed.

My heart was pounding louder than the basketball. Good thing we weren't hurt! I sat up and watched as Matt tried to block the Tiger player's shot.

He jumped very high, but the Tiger jumped higher. When Matt came down, his ankle twisted under him.

Suddenly everyone was quiet—except Matt. He crumpled to the floor and sat there, sobbing and holding his ankle.

I could tell he was hurt . . . and it looked pretty bad.

Chapter 4

"Is he going to be okay?" Mitchell asked.

"I think so," Mom told us. She and Matt's mom, who had been sitting in the bleachers, helped Matt up to his feet. I mean, his foot. The other foot was dangling in the air.

"It hurts, Mom," Matt cried. His face was pale. "Do I have to go to the hospital?"

Mrs. Carter nodded. "But don't

worry, Matt," she said. "Everything will be all right."

We watched Matt and his mother leave the gym. They were in such a hurry, Matt didn't even change out of his uniform.

And when he was out the door, we could still hear him crying.

"Ow," Mitchell said softly. This time he didn't make a joke.

"Matt will miss the brownies after the game," Brenda said sadly. "My dad made them. They're really, really good."

Joanna's eyes filled with tears. "Will they have to cut his foot off?" she asked.

"Sometimes they have to," Alex said. He looked scared. "If his ankle is hurt really badly, they might have to cut off his whole *leg*."

29

"No, they won't do that," Mom reassured Alex and Joanna.

"Matt Carter just got hurt," Danny said into his pretend microphone. "Will the Leftovers' star miss the whole season? Stay tuned."

"Matt is our best player," Josh said. "If he can't play, we can't win."

"We'll never get any more baskets," Lucy added. "But that's okay. We'll just listen to the ball bounce."

"The Leftovers may never score another point!" Danny's eyes opened wide. "You just heard it from Lucy Marcus. Now back to your local news."

"Okay, Rangers," Mom said. "Matt will be all right. Let's score!"

Matt hadn't looked very all right, I thought as I ran onto the court.

I threw the ball to Julie. Julie

30

passed it back to Adam. "Coming through!" Adam yelled, and he dribbled toward the basket as fast as he could.

"Shoot! Shoot! Shoot!" the kids on the bench chanted.

The Tigers were guarding him pretty well, though. Adam dribbled around, trying to find a hole he could go through.

"I'm free!" Julie yelled. She stood

near the basket and waved her arms like crazy.

But Adam didn't even look at her. Instead, he jumped high into the air and let the ball fly.

I held my breath.

"And it's . . ." Danny began. Then he made a face. "Air ball."

"Hair ball," Mitchell said. But I didn't laugh.

"Get closer next time, Adam!" I shouted. It was a pretty dumb play, I thought. He'd been a mile away from the basket.

The Tigers brought the ball down the court and shot. I tried to block it, but I wasn't tall enough. The ball rolled around the rim and dropped into the net. Two more points for the Tigers.

"Come on, Rangers!" Mom yelled.

Lucy passed to Julie, who started dribbling. "Pass, Julie!" Adam yelled.

Julie was too busy watching the ball to look up. "No way!" she said. "You didn't pass to me. Why should I pass to you?"

"Julie!" I shouted. One of the Tigers was running at her.

Julie changed direction and kept dribbling. She still didn't look up.

"Zimmer into the front court!" Danny announced. "Now she dribbles to the side . . . farther . . . farther . . ."

"Julie, stop!" I wailed.

But Julie didn't seem to hear. And the next thing we knew, she had dribbled over the sideline. She was out-of-bounds.

"Julie!" Lucy yelled. I shut my eyes. Julie was dribbling right toward the wall!

The referee blew his whistle. *Tweet!* But Julie kept right on dribbling. If the ball hadn't rolled off her toes, I bet she would have crashed into the side of the gym.

The Tigers had the ball back— again.

"Defense!" Mom told us. I bit my lip. I hoped we could keep the Tigers from scoring.

One of the Tigers dribbled down the floor. He bounced a pass to one of his teammates, and the ball went right in front of me. I took a deep breath and dived.

Ouch!

I got a faceful of floor. But I didn't have the ball.

"Matt would have had that one," Julie said sadly as I picked myself up.

"Yeah," I agreed. I watched the Tigers score again. "He would have gotten to that one."

Adam passed to Danny, who dribbled back and forth. "West has the ball," he announced into his microphone. "The fans go wild!"

"Hey, Danny," Mom shouted from

the bench. "Dribble to t... ...

Danny didn't listen. ... move!" he said. He boun... extra high and spun in a c... he reached for it again—o... ...it him on the shoulder. "Ow!" he shouted.

"Danny West says ow," Mitchell said in a silly announcer voice. "And the fans go wild."

The Tigers got the ball. They scored, of course. When we got the ball back, Julie passed it to Lucy. Lucy passed it to me. I dribbled to the centerline.

"Go, Catherine!" Mom called encouragingly.

I tried to look in front of me, but I couldn't dribble without watching the ball. So I backed up. I didn't want to get hurt like Matt!

35

Antler backs up," Danny said, still pretending to announce the game. "Here come the Tigers!"

Suddenly there were Tigers on all sides of me. "Pass it!" I could hear

PASS IT!

Adam calling. But I couldn't see Adam, so how could I pass it to him? "Help!" I yelled. I turned around a couple of times. Still, the only thing I could see was Tigers.

"Pass it!" Adam's voice seemed very far away.

I felt as though I had run all over the court. All of a sudden I saw a hole between two Tigers. I dribbled through it. And there was the basket!

I shot. The ball soared up—and swished through the net.

"Yeah!" I screamed. I pumped my fist in the air. My first basket!

"Catherine Antler scores," Danny said into the pretend microphone. "For the Tigers!"

For the Tigers? I stared at Danny.

Then I stared at the basket.

"Oh, no!" I whispered. I had thrown the ball into the wrong basket!

I had scored my first points, all right.

For the wrong team!

Chapter 5

"Is your ankle broken, Matt?" Julie wanted to know.

Matt grinned. "Yep," he said, and he made a cracking noise with his tongue. It was the next day, and we were at practice.

I looked at Matt's cast. "Did it hurt?"

"A *lot*," Matt said. "Like someone stuck a knife into me."

"Wow," Brenda said.

"Cool," Adam added.

"It took about six hours for the doctors to look at it," Matt said. "We had to eat potato chips for dinner." He licked his lips. "Potato chips and orange pop."

I remembered what I'd eaten for dinner: tuna fish on toast. Potato chips sounded better. "Can you walk?" I asked.

"Yeah. Want to see?" Matt lurched forward. His cast clunked against the floor.

"Neat," Alex said. He tried to walk the way Matt did, but he fell over instead.

Julie shook her head. "It was just bad luck," she said.

"You mean a bad break," Mitchell said. He laughed. "Bad *break*. Get it?"

It was a bad break for the whole team, I thought. And it had happened so fast—in the middle of the very first game of the season!

Mom blew her whistle. "This drill is called stop-and-pop," she told us when we got to the bench.

"Pop?" Alex frowned. "Like the noise Matt's ankle made when he broke it? It went *pop*. I heard it."

"Not that kind of pop, Alex," Mom told him.

"Pop like the kind Matt drank for dinner last night?" Josh asked. He smacked his lips.

Mom sighed. "No, Josh. In stop-and-pop, you dribble down the floor. When you get close to the basket, you stop—"

"And somebody pops you if you get too close," Mitchell finished. He swung his fist and smacked it into his palm. Then he winked at me.

"Mitchell likes Catherine," I could hear Julie whisper to Joanna. "Mitchell likes Catherine!"

I looked at the ground. I didn't want Julie to say that.

Mom ignored Mitchell. "And then you pop the ball at the basket. Like this. Pop!" She tossed the ball. It missed the hoop by about ten feet. "Of course, you should get closer than I did."

"Oh, that's *easy*," Matt said. "I could do that in my sleep."

We did stop-and-pop for a while. It wasn't easy, at least not for us. Almost all of our shots missed. And most of them didn't even hit the rim.

"Dribble closer to the basket!" Mom kept telling us.

"Aw, that's boring," Matt said. He limped around on his broken ankle. "Shoot from way far away. That's the fun part."

I tried to do what Matt said. But I kept on missing.

"Every time I shoot, the ball goes *there*," Alex said with a sigh. He pointed to a spot five feet left of the basket.

"*I'll* show you," Matt said. He clumped onto the court. "Like this."

He aimed and shot. The ball soared up high. It hit the rim and bounced away.

"Close," I said.

"Yeah." Matt said. "You'd better go get the ball."

"Me?" I asked. "*You* shot it!" Then I remembered. Matt had his ankle in a cast, so he couldn't run.

It must be nice not to have to chase your missed shots, I thought as I ran after the ball. Maybe being in a cast wasn't so bad.

After a few more minutes of stop-and-pop, Mom called us all together. Matt stayed on the court, looking sad. I watched him dribble a few times. Then he took a shot.

Swish! Right into the net.

He was pretty good, I had to admit. In fact, he was the best on our team, even with a broken ankle.

"Stop-and-pop was hard, wasn't it?" Mom asked.

"It was almost impossible, Mrs. Antler," Julie said.

"Matt can do it," Brenda said. "How come Matt can do it and we can't?"

"Matt is very good at making long shots," Mom explained. "The rest of you aren't yet, but that's okay. How can we make shooting easier for you?"

We looked at each other.

"Maybe we could use a ladder," Joanna suggested.

"Or maybe we could shoot the ball from closer in," Danny said.

"Good idea, Danny." Mom was smiling.

"Rat-a-tat-tat!" Mitchell pointed a pretend gun at the basketball. "That's how you shoot a ball." He poked me in the side. "Get it?"

I sighed and stepped away. I like Mitchell. He's funny. But I was getting a little tired of his jokes. And I was getting a lot tired of being jabbed in the side.

Also, I didn't want anybody saying "Mitchell likes Catherine!"

Josh waved his hand. "Some of us have trouble dribbling, too," he said.

Like Alex, I thought. And Yin.

"Like Catherine," Josh said.

"Hey!" I exclaimed. "I can too dribble! At least I got a basket yesterday!"

"Yeah, for the wrong team," Josh replied.

"Dribbling *is* hard," Mom said in a quiet voice. "So how could you get the ball to the basket without dribbling?"

"Climb on each other's shoulders?" Danny suggested.

"Hide the ball under your shirt and run with it," Lucy said.

Alex frowned, then said, "Pass it?"

"Good idea, Alex!" Mom nodded. "I'm going to show you a special play. It's called a fast break." She bounced a ball on the floor.

A fast break? I bit my lip.

That was what had happened to Matt's ankle!

Chapter

6

It turned out that fast breaks don't have anything to do with broken ankles.

Mom sent Yin and Julie across the court. The rest of us stood under the basket. "Matt," Mom called, "would you shoot for us, please?"

Matt clunked over. He was eating a brownie! I was jealous. Brenda's dad had made us another batch, but we didn't usually get brownies till practice was over. "Sure, Mrs. Antler," he said.

He made the shot, too.

Mitchell picked up the ball. "Do I dribble?" he asked.

Mom shook her head. "Pass it to Julie and Yin," she said.

"I get it!" Joanna said. "They'll be the only ones there. They'll grab it and—"

"And put it into the net," Adam finished.

"Rubin goes for the fast break!" Danny shouted as Mitchell threw the ball toward Yin. It bounced a few times. Then it rolled. Finally it stopped.

The ball never did get to Yin and Julie.

"Let's try again," Mom said. She sent Alex and Josh down the court. Matt shot another basket, and Joanna got the ball.

She threw it hard, all right.

It bounced out-of-bounds and hit the bench.

"Oops!" Joanna said.

"Fast breaks don't work," Lucy said. "We should try slow breaks."

"Yeah," Mitchell agreed. "I'd rather have breakfast than a fast break. Get it?"

"Lucy! Mitchell!" Mom called. "It's your turn!"

"Time for a slow break," Mitchell said. He grabbed Lucy's hand, and they ran across the court as if they were in slow motion.

I wrinkled my nose. I didn't want anyone to say Mitchell was my boyfriend. But why did he have to grab Lucy's hand like that?

Matt shot. Danny passed. And this time the ball went where it was supposed to.

Too bad Lucy wasn't watching.

Thump! The ball hit her in the back.

"Ow!" Lucy cried. She rubbed her back where the ball had hit. "Mrs.

Antler, I think my back is broken!"

It wasn't. But Mom told her to sit on the bench until she felt better. Lucy walked over and grabbed a brownie, then sat down.

Julie saw the brownie, too. "Mrs. Antler, I split my nail. May I be excused?"she asked. Mom nodded, and off Julie went to the bench.

"Mrs. Antler!" Josh's hand shot up in the air. "I don't feel so good. I might throw up."

"Oh, dear." Mom frowned. "I guess you'd better go sit down, too. Brenda! Your turn to be under the basket."

I threw the ball to Brenda. Brenda shot—but she couldn't score. She tried again. No luck. She was just too short.

Brenda sighed. She tossed the ball up and hit it with her forehead, just like a soccer player.

Bad move! She had forgotten that basketballs are very heavy and hard.

"Ow!" Brenda grabbed her head. "I think I put a hole in my skull!"

"Really?" Alex looked scared. "Are your brains going to fall out?"

"Of course not, Alex," Mom said. "Go rest for a while, Brenda."

Brenda smiled and skipped over to the bench. "Pass me a brownie, guys!" she said when she got there.

She didn't look as if her head hurt a lot. But then, the other kids didn't look hurt or sick, either. Josh had brownie crumbs around his mouth. And Lucy was doing handstands against the wall of the gym. They were all laughing.

"Catherine!" Mom called. "Go under the basket!"

I frowned. I probably wouldn't be

able to catch the ball anyway. And if I did, I didn't think I would score.

"I love your dad's brownies, Brenda," Josh said. "I'm going to have three!"

"Catherine!" Mom shouted again.

I made up my mind. I took a step and pretended to fall. "Ow!" I yelled, grabbing my wrist.

"Oh, Catherine," Mom sighed. "Are you all right?"

"Not really," I said. I shut my eyes and moaned. "I'd better sit out for a little while—okay?"

But I didn't wait for her to answer.

I ran right to the bench—and the brownies!

Chapter

7

"Catherine!" Matt was shouting.

"What is it?" I asked. It was the next day, and we were practicing for our game against the White Sox.

"Would you get my ball for me?" Matt pointed at a ball rolling across the court.

I wanted to say, "Get it yourself! I'm busy now!" But I didn't. Instead, I thought about Matt's ankle and how he couldn't walk very well.

I sighed. "Okay, Matt."

It took a while to get Matt's ball, because it had rolled under the bleachers. "What are you doing, anyway?" I asked Matt when I brought it back to him.

"I'm trying to spin the ball on my finger," he told me. He set the ball on his fingertip and spun it. "See?"

The ball slid off. It rolled toward the basket.

"Oh, well," Matt said with a sigh. "Hey, Catherine, would you get it?"

I got the ball for Matt. But I wished I hadn't.

"Matt is getting to be a pain in the neck," I said to Lucy a couple of minutes later.

"Yeah." Lucy nodded. "He's lucky he got hurt. I wish I were hurt, too."

"Really?" I asked.

"Well, not really hurt," Lucy said. "But it would be fun to wear a cast. Do you think they would put a cast on me even if I didn't break my ankle?"

I scratched my head. "I don't think so," I told her.

But she was right. It *would* be fun to have a cast. It *would* be fun to spin balls and not have to get them when they rolled away.

It might be more fun than playing basketball.

Matt grabbed one of Mr. Bailey's brownies.

It might be a *lot* more fun, I thought. I licked my lips.

"Look at me!" Lucy said. She walked with a limp. "Ow, ow, ow. I hurt my ankle!"

"For real?" I asked.

"No, for pretend," Lucy answered in a whisper. "But don't tell anyone."

I grinned. We both limped to the bench. "Mom?" I said. "Lucy and I think our ankles are broken!"

Mom bent down and touched my ankle.

"Ow!" I yelled. I breathed really hard, the way Matt had.

"Hmm." Mom stood back up and frowned. "Which ankle did you break?"

"This one," I said, holding out my right foot. Wait a minute, I thought. Maybe I had been limping with my left foot instead. "I mean, this one." I switched feet.

Mom shook her head. "Nice try, girls," she said. "But you can't fool me!

NO FAIR

Now go shoot a few more baskets."

When the game started, Matt stood on the sidelines and spun his ball. Except sometimes he couldn't hold on. Twice the referee had to stop the game so someone could get Matt's ball.

"It's not fair," Brenda said. We were sitting on the bench. "Just because Matt is hurt, he gets all the good luck."

"Yeah," Danny said. "No one would let *us* spin a ball on our fingertips."

Julie nodded. "Mrs. Antler would say, 'Julie, stop it!'"

I smiled. She sounded just like Mom.

"Come on, Leftovers!" Matt yelled. He bounced his ball on the floor. "Shoot the ball, Alex! Don't be a wimp!"

Alex took a deep breath and shot.

It went about five feet to the left of the basket—just like all of Alex's shots. A White Sox player grabbed it.

"Alex!" Joanna moaned. "Why did you shoot?"

Alex turned red. "Because I'm—" he began.

He didn't finish, but I knew what he'd been about to say: "Because I'm not a wimp!"

"*I* would have scored on that shot," Matt boasted, and he bounced his ball even harder.

He probably would have, too, I thought.

"Pass the ball, Rangers!" Mom cried.

"Pass?" Matt said softly. "What's the fun of *that*?"

The White Sox scored. Joanna took

the ball down the court. She dribbled this way and that. "Go, Joanna!" I shouted.

"Go, Joanna!" Julie echoed.

Joanna bounced the ball and ran as fast as she could. Her braids bounced all over the place. Then she stopped and held the ball. Her braids stopped bouncing, too.

"Pass!" I started to say. But I changed my mind. I didn't want Matt to think—well, you know.

"I'm going to score!" Joanna yelled. She jumped and threw the ball toward the hoop.

"Oops," Julie said quietly.

I sighed. The ball hadn't gone anywhere near the basket. Joanna had shot from way too far away.

And the White Sox had the ball again.

Over and over, we would try to dribble down the court. But whenever someone would try to pass, Matt would make a face. "I could have scored from there," he'd say. "Passing is for losers!"

After a while we just plain stopped passing. After all, who wants to be called a loser and a wimp?

"Why is Matt being so mean?" I asked Mom on the way home from the game. We had lost, 26–6.

"Mean?" Mom's eyebrows went up. "How is he being mean?"

"Well, he keeps calling us wimps," I explained. "And he tells us to shoot from too far away, and then he gets mad when we don't score."

And he got to eat three brownies, I thought. And he spins the ball on his finger, too. But I didn't say that part.

Mom looked at me thoughtfully.

"Do you have to do what he says?" she asked.

I bit my lip. "I guess not," I said. "But—"

"Matt loves basketball," Mom went on. "What if you'd been the one who got hurt? How would you feel?"

"I wouldn't mind," I said. "Not much." Eating Mr. Bailey's brownies was more fun than playing basketball.

Mom grinned. "Well, maybe *you* wouldn't mind," she said. "But Matt does. He hates not being able to play." She turned the car onto our street. "When people don't get to do what they really love to do, they don't always act nice."

I thought about what Mom had said.

It made some sense.

Kind of.

Chapter 8

"Tigers rule! Tigers rule!" the Tigers shouted. It was a couple of days later, and we were about to play them again.

"They mean, Tigers *drool*!" Mitchell said.

Yin grinned. "Tigers drool!" she shouted.

Mom frowned when she heard that. "Why don't you cheer for your own team instead?"

"Why should we do that, Mrs. Antler?" Alex asked. He had a sad look on his face. "I mean, we're not very good or anything."

"We'll probably lose," Julie said.

Mitchell took off his shoe and put it to his ear. "The aliens say we're going to lose, too," he reported.

Mom grinned. "Well, the aliens are wrong this time. We're not going to lose, because we have a secret weapon," she said. "Presenting . . . Matt! Ta-da!"

I stared at Matt. How could he be a secret weapon when he was wearing a cast?

"Matt is my assistant coach today," Mom went on. "He'll tell you when to pass the ball."

Danny raised his hand. "He'll never say a word, Mrs. Antler!"

63

"Matt hates passing," Joanna added.

"He used to," Mom said. "But not anymore." She smiled. "You see, I made a new rule. After the game, we're all going to split two of Mr. Bailey's brownies."

"Just two?" Danny looked disgusted.

I made a face. That would be only a tiny little bit for each of us.

"No fair!" Joanna cried.

Mom held up her hand. "But whenever somebody scores, we add two more to split."

"Two more for every basket?" Brenda asked. She smacked her lips.

"That's right," Mom said. "But it counts only if the person who gets the points hasn't scored yet."

I thought about it. If we each scored a basket, then we would get 22 brownies. With the 2 we would get anyway, that made 24 brownies—2 each.

I could almost taste them.

"But what if we don't score any points?" Adam asked.

Mom shrugged. "Then you get just two brownies to share among the twelve of you."

"Well, I want more," Brenda cried. "Rangers rule!"

"Rangers rule!" we all shouted.

The game got off to a good start. Joanna dribbled the ball toward the Tigers' basket. One of the Tigers tried to steal the ball, but he missed. "Shoot!" Alex called to her.

But Matt's voice was louder. "Pass it to Danny, Joanna!" he yelled and pointed.

There was Danny, standing under the basket. Matt was exactly right.

Danny was wide open. Joanna passed. The ball bounced off the floor and into Danny's arms.

"Shoot!" Matt yelled.

Danny shot. It bounced off the backboard and went in.

"Four brownies!" Brenda announced, smiling.

I could see a grin on Matt's face, too.

The next time we had the ball, Danny dribbled almost to the basket. He could have scored again—maybe.

But we wouldn't have gotten more brownies that way.

I guess Matt was thinking the same

thing. "Pass!" he shouted. "Pass to Julie!"

"West passes to Zimmer," Danny said as he threw the ball to Julie. She whirled and tossed it toward the basket. "And it's . . . good!" he yelled into his pretend microphone.

"Six brownies," Brenda told us.

A little later Mitchell got a basket. "Yeah!" Matt shouted.

"Rangers rule!" Mitchell yelled. "I mean, Rangers *cool*! Rangers cool!"

He winked at me. And I winked back. I didn't care what anybody said. The Rangers really *were* cool!

½ Time

At the beginning of the second half I scored. Then Adam scored. That was eighteen brownies so far. Everyone had scored except Alex, Lucy, and Brenda.

Uh-oh, I thought. Alex, Lucy, and Brenda were our worst basketball players. Alex kept shooting five feet to the left of the basket. Brenda couldn't throw the ball high enough. And Lucy was never looking when we passed to her.

The Tigers scored. Then they scored again. With three minutes left, they tied the game. Then they were ahead.

"Too bad," Mom sighed. "Go, Rangers!"

Julie made a face. "I told you we would lose," she said.

Danny dribbled down the court. Three Tigers surrounded him.

"Pass it!" Matt yelled.

Danny glanced around and saw

that Alex was open. "Alex!" Danny shouted, and he passed.

Alex grabbed the ball. Then he looked at the basket.

I wanted him to shoot. If he scored, we'd get two more brownies—and the game would be tied.

I just hoped he could get the ball in the basket for once.

Alex jumped up. Just as he was about to release the ball, a Tiger hit his wrist. "Ow!" Alex yelled.

The referee blew his whistle. "Foul! Two free throws for Alex!"

Alex held his wrist and blinked hard. Then he took the ball and went to the free-throw line.

"Come on, Alex!" Matt shouted. He stamped the foot with the cast on it.

Alex took a deep breath. His face looked as though his wrist was hurting.

He bounced the ball once and then shot. As usual, the ball went about five feet to the left of the net.

"Oh, no," Julie sighed.

"Hey, Alex!" Matt cried suddenly. "Pretend the net is over here!" He hobbled over and stood about five feet to the *right* of the basket.

Of course! I thought. Alex's shots always curved. Matt was trying to make them curve *into* the basket.

"Good plan, Matt!" I yelled.

Alex threw the ball as hard as he could toward Matt—and it landed in the basket!

"Twenty brownies!" Brenda cheered.

And now we were losing by just one point!

Chapter 9

The Tigers had the ball. They dribbled and passed.

"Get the ball, Catherine!" Mom shouted.

I lunged at the boy with the ball. But I missed and crashed to the floor. "Ow!" I cried.

"Time-out!" The referee blew his whistle.

"Are you okay?" Mom said, dashing to my side.

My leg hurt. But I didn't want to come out of the game—not when we were so close to winning. I bit my lip so I wouldn't cry. "I'm all right," I said.

"Tigers' ball," said the referee. "Go!"

The Tigers passed and dribbled, dribbled and passed. I looked around for my teammates. I saw Brenda, Danny, Alex, and—

Where was Lucy?

I couldn't find her anywhere.

There were just thirty seconds left in the game. We had to score again to win.

"Get the ball!" Matt hollered.

Twenty seconds!

The tallest girl on the Tigers dribbled toward the basket.

Fifteen seconds!

Danny dived for the ball and

grabbed it away from her! "West with the steal!" he yelled. Then he started to dribble toward the basket.

I looked at the clock. There were only ten seconds left now. I didn't think Danny could get to the basket in time.

"Fast break!" Matt shouted. He cupped his hands around his mouth so Danny would hear him. "Fast break!"

Fast break! Of course! And at that moment I saw Lucy.

She was lying under the basket at the other end of the court, her ear to the floor.

"Lucy!" I yelled.

Danny pulled his arm back. "West goes for the fast break!" he announced. Then he let the ball fly. It sailed over our heads, then hit the floor and bounced—once, twice, three times.

"Lucy!" Adam screamed.

Lucy sat up. "Who's that dribbling

over my bridge?" she asked in a troll voice. Then she stared in surprise as the ball bounced right into her lap.

"Shoot it!" Joanna yelled at the top of her lungs.

Slowly Lucy stood up. She threw the ball in the air as we held our breath.

And then—

Just as the last second ticked off the clock—

The ball flew through the net!

"Two points!" Danny jumped into the air, a big grin on his face. "The Leftovers win it, 21–20, on a last-second shot by Lucy Marcus!"

"That's twenty-two brownies!" Brenda informed us.

"I had another message from the aliens," Mitchell said. "They changed their minds. They said we would win after all."

We all cheered. It felt good to win. And it felt good that everyone had scored. Even Alex. Even Lucy—

I frowned. "Brenda," I said. "Brenda didn't score."

Brenda shrugged. "Oh, that's okay," she said. "We won. And I'd have to be taller to get any points, anyway."

Suddenly I remembered something Danny had said. Something about standing on each other's shoulders. . . .

"Hey, Mom," I said. "If we can help Brenda score a basket now, do we get two extra brownies?"

Mom nodded.

So Adam, Mitchell, Joanna, and I stood side by side. And Danny, Julie, and Lucy hopped onto our shoulders.

"Careful," Mom warned. But there was a twinkle in her eye.

"We will," I promised.

Josh and Yin boosted Brenda so that she was on the very top row. Then Alex held her in place while Matt gave her a basketball.

Brenda aimed carefully and then threw the ball hard. It sailed up . . . and then swished down through the net.

"Two points!" Danny shouted.

And we got two brownies each after all.

THE LEFTOVERS

by Tristan Howard

Don't be left out!

The Leftovers are the wackiest team in any league.
No matter what the sport, fun and laughs are always
part of the game plan.

BASEBALL:

❑ BBS56923-6   **The Leftovers #1: Strike Out!** $2.99

❑ BBS56924-4   **The Leftovers #2: Catch Flies!** $2.99

SOCCER:

❑ BBS89896-5   **The Leftovers #3: Use Their Heads!** $2.99

❑ BBS92133-9   **The Leftovers #4: Reach Their Goal!** $2.99

BASKETBALL:

❑ BBS96219-1   **The Leftovers #5: Fast Break!** $3.50

❑ BBS96221-3   **The Leftovers #6: Get Jammed!** $3.50

Available wherever you buy books or use this order form.

- -

Send orders to:
Scholastic Inc., P.O. Box 7502, 2931 East McCarty Street, Jefferson City, MO 65102

Please send me the books I have checked above. I am enclosing $_____ (please add $2.00 to cover
shipping and handling). Send check or money order—no cash or C.O.D.s please.

Name_____**Birthdate**_____

Address_____

City_____**State**_____**Zip**_____

Please allow four to six weeks for delivery. Offer good in U.S. only. Sorry mail orders are not available to residents of
Canada. Prices subject to change.

LO796